I was eating my lunch
Rabbit when Prissy came into the utility
room.

I still find it hard to believe what she did
next.

She bent down behind me and pulled my
tail, very hard. I yowled, I admit it, and
Miles came running in from the kitchen.

"I never!" said Prissy. "I never pulled
Blossom's tail."

"You did, didn't you?" Miles said. "I
know you did."

"I never!" wailed Prissy.

"What's all that noise?" Mum said.
"Come in here at once, Miles, and stop
shouting at poor little Prissy."

"But, Mum," Miles said. "She pulled
Blossom's tail."

"Nonsense," said Mum. "I'm sure she'd
never do anything like that . . ."

Blossom's Revenge is the first title in a series
about a group of cats who are good friends,
the Cats of Cuckoo Square.

N

Don't miss any of the titles in this enchanting series about a group of cats, the Cats of Cuckoo Square.

Available now from Young Corgi Books:

BLOSSOM'S REVENGE
PICASSO PERKINS
CALLIE'S KITTEN
GEEJAY, THE HERO

Blossom's Revenge

BLOSSOM'S REVENGE
A YOUNG CORGI BOOK: 0 552 52972 9

First publication in Great Britain

PRINTING HISTORY
Young Corgi edition published 1997

3 5 7 9 10 8 6 4

Copyright © 1997 by Adèle Geras
Illustrations copyright © 1997 by Tony Ross

Set in 17/21pt Bembo Schoolbook
by Phoenix Typesetting, Ilkley, West Yorkshire

Young Corgi Books are published by Transworld Publishers,
61–63 Uxbridge Road, London W5 5SA,
a division of The Random House Group Ltd,
in Australia by Random House Australia (Pty) Ltd,
20 Alfred Street, Milsons Point, NSW 2061, Australia,
in New Zealand by Random House New Zealand Ltd,
18 Poland Road, Glenfield, Auckland 10, New Zealand
and in South Africa by Random House (Pty) Ltd,
Endulini, 5a Jubilee Road, Parktown 2193, South Africa.

Printed and bound in Great Britain by
CPI Antony Rowe, Eastbourne

THE CATS OF CUCKOO SQUARE

Blossom's Revenge

ADÈLE GERAS

Illustrated by Tony Ross

YOUNG CORGI BOOKS

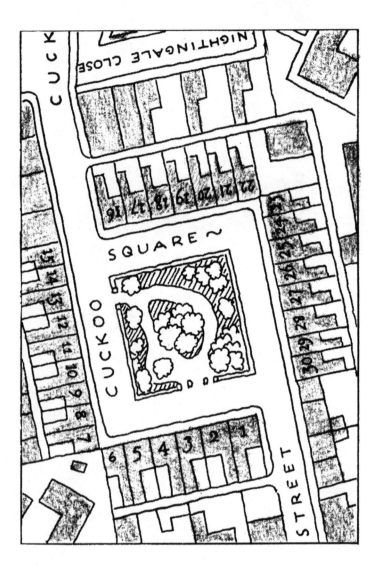

1 Prissy Arrives...

"Look at that cat!" said Prissy
Pinkerton. "Why is it so fat?"

Honestly! I had never been so
insulted in my life! I may not be as
slim as I once was, but no-one could
possibly call me *fat*!

Prissy Pinkerton is a very nasty
little girl. She doesn't look nasty. If
you could see her, you would almost

certainly say: "How sweet!" She is six years old. She has curly golden hair. She wears white socks. She sucks her thumb. Her cheeks are dimpled. Her eyes are blue. Nevertheless, she is nasty. I knew she was nasty the moment she opened her mouth to speak.

My name is Blossom and I'm one of the Cuckoo Square Cats. There's a garden in the Square, with railings all around it, and a gate that's kept locked. The flower-beds are well-dug, and there are plenty of shrubs under whose branches we can hide. We like sharpening our claws on the trees, although it is only young kittens who go scrabbling up to the topmost branches, just for the fun of it. My friends and I are too old for that sort of behaviour. We sit on the

benches, or flop about on the soft grass in the summer. The humans have keys to what we cats call Our Place, because we are the ones who use it most often.

My particular friends are Perkins (whose people are the Blythes at number 27), Callie (from number 18) and Geejay (whose real name is Ginger Jack, and who curls up in front of the fire at number 2). Perkins is a large, dignified tabby who has lived in the Square longer than any of us,

Callie is a sweet-
natured, gentle calico
cat with white fur
prettily spotted in
ginger and

black, and Geejay looks like a lion.
He has yellow eyes, and is the best
hunter in the Square.

As for me, I'm fluffy and black
and white, and I like to go through
life as calmly and peacefully
as I can.

Other cats come and go, and we allow them to walk through the Square, but only on their way to somewhere else. This is our territory. This is where we come to get away from our humans, to exchange news, and especially to tell stories.

Earlier today, we were all waiting for the Pinkertons to arrive at my house with their little daughter.

"She is a relation," I told them. "Her name is Prissy. Her parents are bringing her to stay with us for the summer holidays, while they find a new house and get it ready. She's supposed to be company for Miles."

Perkins opened one eye and announced, "Visitors never turn out to be what you think. We have them all the time." He yawned. "Wake me up when she arrives. I do not like to miss anything, but it is hard to keep one's eyes open."

"Perhaps," Callie murmured, "she'll be a lovely little girl."

Callie expects the best of everyone.

I, also, thought it would be delightful to have another child in our house. My people are called Mr and Mrs Randall, but I call them Mum and Dad, because that is Miles's name for them. They are good humans,

although they have their faults.
Mum is house-proud. She prowls
through rooms, armed with a
fearsome device called a Hoover,
which sucks dirt out of the carpet
and makes a most distressing noise.

When I was a kitten, I thought the Hoover was a monster, and hid from it under the chest of drawers, but I'm used to it now. Mum has a long metal tube which she attaches to the Hoover sometimes.
"This is my Dustbuster, Blossom," she told me once. "It works wonders with cat hairs."

Whenever Mum mentions cat hairs, I yawn. She goes on and on about them. They are her favourite subject. She ought to be grateful that

I am black and white. I leave pale hairs on the dark things and dark hairs on the pale things, and this allows her to play happily with her Dustbuster almost every day.

Dad is a little absent-minded. Sometimes he doesn't notice me. He has sat on me, tripped over me, and even driven off in his car while I was curled up asleep on the bonnet.

"He likes you when he *does* see you," Miles tells me, and I'm sure that's true, but Dad's mind is often on other things. Also, he wears glasses which are supposed to help him to see better, but sometimes he puts them down and forgets where they are.

It is Miles who is my special friend. He is eight years old and he loves me. I know, because he tells me so. I wish I could have a prawn for every time he's said, "You're our best and most beautiful Blossom in the world."

When the Randalls talked about their niece, Prissy, I thought, "What a silly name!"

It turned out to be short for

Priscilla, but that didn't make it any better.

"Why does she have to come here?" Miles asked at breakfast one day.

"Well," said Mum, "Iris *is* my sister, and blood is thicker than water."

"What does that mean?" Miles asked.

"It means," said Dad gloomily, "that our lives are going to be turned upside down."

"Nonsense!" said Mum. "She's only six. What could she possibly do?"

I told the Cuckoo Square Cats what Mum had said as we waited for the Pinkertons' car.

Perkins sighed. "In my experience," he said, licking his left front paw, "the younger the child, the more things it finds to do, not all of them pleasant, I assure you."

"Look!" said Geejay, who was perched on the lowest branch of a tree. "Here comes a car I've never seen before. Is it them?"

"These humans go so fast," said Callie. "I wish they wouldn't. It gets my fur in a flurry."

I peered out from between the railings. A car was indeed coming up to the Randalls' front door, looking and sounding like some roaring, glittering beast. Three people got out of it, and went up the steps to my house. One of them was a little girl.

"I shall go and introduce myself,"
I said to my friends. "It's good
manners."

"She looks so pretty!" said Callie.

She did, but, as I have already
said, her very first words made me
realize how unkind she really was.

After saying I was fat she went on,
"I *hate* fat cats!"

In my opinion, it's extremely
impolite to say you hate a fellow
creature.

"At least," I said to my friends,
"Miles loves me exactly as I am."

And it's true. "We'd never swap
you," he tells me, "for any scrawny,
skinny, mangy old THIN cat . . .
you're our Blossom Butterball.
You're beautiful."

I try to be modest about it, but it *is* true that in my younger days, everyone who saw me said I was a splendid creature. I am proud of my eyes, which are like green jewels: emeralds perhaps or clear, pale jade.

I crept round everyone's legs and waited for Mum and Dad to open the door. There was much squawking and kissing and shouts of "Iris!" and "Darling!" and "How lovely!" and "Prissy, how sweet you look!" I have never understood why humans make such a to-do about greeting one another. A great deal of time could be saved if they simply touched noses from time to time, as we do.

"Look!" said Prissy. "Flowers!"
She bent down to pick a geranium
from one of the big flowerpots
(Mum's pride and joy) standing
beside the front door.

I could see that Mum was not
pleased at all. She put her hand on
Prissy's shoulder and said, "Please
don't do that, dear. The flowers look
so pretty where they are. Come
inside and have a drink."

I don't think anyone but me noticed how Prissy pressed her lips together and narrowed her eyes. She was obviously a child who liked her own way.

"Come along, darling," her mother said. "Let's get these cases indoors."

Prissy seemed to have a lot of luggage for a small child.

"I'll take these two," said Uncle Cliff, Prissy's father.

"But I want to bring something!" said the dainty little thing, and I could see her bottom lip begin to tremble. Later, I learned that when Prissy said "I want", trouble was never very far away.

Uncle Cliff said, "Right, then. You bring in that small one."

I was behind Prissy, and saw exactly what she did when no-one was looking. The grown-ups had gone into the hall. Prissy picked up her suitcase and accidentally-on-purpose, as Miles would say, swung round so that a corner of the case knocked one of the flowerpots over. It went flying down the front steps, shattering into a thousand fragments and leaving bits of earth and torn

petals everywhere. Prissy giggled and muttered something under her breath.

I saw her satisfied smirk, but no-one else did. I stared at the child, and she glared back at me. She had certainly seen me looking at her.

"Go away, horrid cat!" she said. "I'm going to call my mummy and I know what I'm going to say." Then she yelled "Mummee!" so loudly that my fur stood on end. Her mother and father came out, closely followed by the Randalls.

"Oh, dear," said Auntie Iris. "Whatever happened?"

"That cat," said Prissy. "It scared me. It made me swing my case and then the pot got hit."

If there is one thing all cats hate, it is being called 'it'.

"Never worry, old sport," boomed Uncle Cliff. "We'll pay for the damage . . . good as new in no time, eh?"

"I'll get a broom," said Mum. She

was upset, I could see. "You all go in for a cup of tea."

I went back to Perkins, Callie and Geejay, who had been watching the drama unfold.

"Did you see what she did?" I asked them. My fur was still standing on end from the injustice of it all. "She blamed *me*! How dare she?"

"That child," said Perkins, "is nothing but trouble, mark my words."

"Perhaps," said Callie, "it was just an accident."

"If that was an accident," said Geejay, "my tail's a feather-duster!"

2 From Bad to Worse...

Prissy Pinkerton did not get better.
After her parents left, she got worse.

"They've given her my room,
Blossom," said Miles. "I've got to
sleep in the spare room. She's
allowed to play with all my stuff."

I rubbed my head against his
hand, to express my sympathy. Prissy
had been upsetting me, too. It's a

tradition in the Randall house that we all sit down to breakfast together. There are four chairs round the kitchen table, one for each of the humans and one for me. I like listening to Dad reading snippets of news from the paper (if he hasn't lost his glasses) and Miles gives me his buttery knife to lick when Mum's back is turned. On her first morning in our house, Prissy came down to breakfast and took no notice of the extra chair Mum had brought in for her from the hall. I had been asleep, but opened one eye when Prissy came into the room. The next thing that happened felt to me like an earthquake.

"Off! Off, cat," she giggled and

she tipped my chair violently
forward, so that I slid to the floor in
a muddle, with my heart beating so
loudly from the dreadful shock that I
was surprised no-one else could hear
it. I went off with my tail swishing
behind me to show how angry I
was, and sat on the window-seat,
wishing I was the sort of cat who
enjoyed scratching people.

"That's Blossom's chair!" Miles was indignant.

"It's my chair now," said Prissy and sat down firmly. "Where's the apple juice?"

"There's orange juice or milk," Mum cooed soothingly.

"I want apple juice!" Prissy said.

"We'll get some when we go shopping. Have some cereal . . . here."

"I like Poppycrunch!"

"We haven't got Poppycrunch,"
said Mum. "We'll get some. We'll go
to the shops straight after breakfast."

Prissy picked up a piece of toast
and left the room nibbling it.

"Poor little thing!" said Mum to
Dad. "I expect she's missing her
parents."

When Mum and Miles and Prissy
had left for the shops, I went into the
Square, to see if my friends were in
the garden. I found Callie stretched
out under a hydrangea bush.

She opened one eye and said,
"You don't look a bit happy,
Blossom."

"I was tipped out of my chair this
morning. That hasn't happened to

me for years. In the Randall house, cats have equal rights to chairs. No-one would dream of tipping me off."

"Really?" said Callie. "That's very unusual, you know. Most humans remove cats from anything they want to sit on, though it's true there are ways and ways of doing it. Prissy could have picked you up kindly and settled you somewhere else. There's no need for tipping."

Later that afternoon, Prissy said to Miles, "Miles, play with me. I want to play."

"How nice, dear," said Mum. "Your cousin wants to play with you. I'll go and start supper."

She left the lounge, and Miles and

Prissy were alone – except for me, of course. I was curled up on my part of the sofa, wide awake, ears wide open, but eyes half closed.

"Let's play Princesses," said Prissy. "You can be my coachman, and . . ." (she turned her twinkly little eyes on me) "you can be the Royal Pet, and sit on this cushion."

"No, she can't," said Miles. "That's my mum's best cushion."

"I say she can," Prissy pouted, and she scooped me up, lifted me into the air, and was about to plonk me down on the cushion. I do not like being picked up. I am too old for it. I do not like playing games, either, so I wriggled out of her grasp. I admit my claws were out, and I

suppose I might *just* have snagged
Prissy's finger with one of them.

She dropped me to the floor and began to shriek. "Auntieee! It's scratched me! There's blood! Horrible cat! Bad cat! Shoo! Go away!" She aimed a kick at me, but I managed to slip behind the sofa.

"Oh, darling!" Mum said, running into the room. "What's Blossom done, then? Come on, Blossom, where are you hiding? This isn't a bit like you!"

You should have seen the fuss! The running around in search of plasters! The fetching of Dettol and cotton wool! The tears! The sweeties to stop the tears! It was almost supper-time when the scene was over, and by then Prissy no longer felt like playing Princesses.

"I want to draw," she said. "I want to do a picture."

"OK," said Miles. "You go up. I'm coming."

When she'd gone, he bent down to stroke me.

"It wasn't your fault, Blossom. She's awful."

I purred at him, to show I agreed.

"Now I've got to go and watch her leaving the tops off my felt-tip pens." He sighed as he left the room.

3. The Ghost Cat

"I wish Prissy Pinkerton," I told the Cuckoo Square Cats, "would just go away. She is a thorough nuisance."

"Many children," said Perkins, "are nuisances. You should make yourself scarce. That's what I do. We have a shed in our garden that's most convenient for that purpose."

"But Miles likes to talk to me," I

said. "He and I know what Prissy is *really* like. Mum and Dad keep patting her on the head and telling Miles to be kind to her, as she's missing her parents. Last night, she had Mum rushing up and down the stairs for ages with glasses of water and slices of apple, and this morning a dreadful thing happened in the bathroom."

"Tell us about it," said Callie.
Geejay wasn't really listening. He
had his eye on a squirrel under one
of the benches.

"I sometimes have my morning
snooze there," I said. "It has a
particularly soft carpet. This morning
I was asleep when that dreadful
child Prissy came in to wash. I
thought I was hidden behind the
clothes-basket, but she must have
seen my tail peeping out, because
she started talking to me."

"That's better than tipping you off chairs and shouting at you," said Callie.

"Not really," I told her. "Not when you hear what she said. She said, 'I can see you, fat cat, and I'm going to pay you back for scratching me. You watch.' I made myself as small as I could, curling up tight with my tail tucked well in. Prissy knelt down near the sink. 'Look, fat cat,' she said. 'You've sat on the toothpaste tube and squashed it because you're so fat, and now see the mess.'

"She squeezed the tube and trailed

sticky white stuff all over the carpet.
Then she shook out a blizzard of
talcum powder and said, 'And you
spilt the powder, too. You're a bad
cat and I'm going to tell on you.'

She left the room, and I could hear her calling from the top of the stairs, 'Auntie! Blossom's messed up the bathroom. Come and see!'

"Mum has only to hear the word 'mess' and she's there in an instant.

"'Oh, Blossom,' she wailed when she saw the state of the carpet. 'What *has* got into you? Downstairs this minute. Go on. Go. I'm very cross with you.'

"I streaked past her legs as quickly as I could, but my paws were covered in talcum powder and I've spent ages trying to lick it off. Have you ever tasted it? I feel quite ill!"

"It's disgusting," said Perkins. "I recommend a cooling drink."

"I had one," I said. "I finished all the water in my bowl, but I'm a little peckish now."

I said goodbye to my friends and padded into the house, wondering which of the tins in my own little cupboard Mum would have opened for my lunch.

I was eating my lunch of Purrfect
Liver and Rabbit when Prissy came
into the utility room.

I still find it hard to believe what
she did next.

She bent down behind me and
pulled my tail, very hard. I yowled, I
admit it, and Miles came running in
from the kitchen.

"I never!" said Prissy. "I never pulled Blossom's tail."

"You did, didn't you?" Miles said. "I know you did."

"I never!" wailed Prissy.

"What's all that noise?" Mum said. "Come in here at once, Miles, and stop shouting at poor little Prissy."

"But, Mum," Miles said. "She pulled Blossom's tail."

"Nonsense," said Mum. "I'm sure she'd never do anything like that. She probably trod on it by accident. It's a very long and bushy tail."

Well, I was happy to hear that my tail was properly appreciated, but I was beginning to wonder whether Miles and I should teach Prissy a lesson.

After lunch, he said to me, "Don't worry, Blossom. I've got ever such a good idea. I'm going to tell Prissy a special story this afternoon. Make sure you come and hear it."

At about five o'clock, the children were sitting on the sofa watching TV.

"Have you ever heard the story,

Prissy," Miles said, "about the ghost that haunts this house?"

"Doesn't," said Prissy, but her mouth was hanging open.

"It does. Listen. Once upon a time, long ago before we started living here, there was this girl."

"What was she called?" Prissy wanted to know.

"Mary," said Miles. "She had a cat called Tom."

I didn't think they were the most exciting names he could have chosen, but they must have been the first ones that popped into his head. I don't think he was expecting Prissy to be asking questions.

"Stop asking me things and just listen," he said. "Mary was so horrid to her cat that he ran away and got run over by a car."

I shivered. This is the fate that we cats fear most.

"Anyway," Miles continued, "Tom's ghost comes back to this house whenever there's a girl here. It's looking for Mary, but it's not good at telling one girl from another, so it'll probably come and haunt you. It's white and terrifying

and it meows in a specially howly
and scary way, and all its fur sticks
out and its eyes glow in the dark
and what it does is, it waits till
you're in bed, then it jumps on top
of you and digs its claws into the
duvet."

"There's no such thing as ghosts,"
said Prissy, but she ran out of the
room looking very nervous.

"Right," said Miles, when she'd gone. "You're going to be the Ghost-Cat of Cuckoo Square. Can you howl like a banshee?"

I spent the next hour or so in the Square, where my friends were full of good advice about how to turn myself into a blood-curdling phantom.

"I was quite a yowler and a howler in my youth," said Perkins. "Listen to this." The sound he made flattened my ears against my skull.

"I couldn't do that!" I said.

"You have to practise," said Perkins. "Try it."

So I opened my mouth as wide as I could, and the noise that came out didn't sound as embarrassing as it might have done. I was obviously a very quick learner.

"Well done!" said Perkins. "Do that a few times and you'll be splendid."

"But you must learn to move like a ghost-cat, too," said Geejay. "No use plodding about sedately."

I sniffed. "I do *not* plod," I said.

"No, no, of course not," said Geejay hastily. "But you must creep menacingly, like this. Look."

He stretched his body out to its full length, crouched very close to the ground and slunk along among the bushes like a tiger.

"I don't think" I said, "that the plumper sort of cat can manage to slink like that."

"I think you should try arching your back and spitting," Callie suggested. "That can be very scary sometimes."

Everyone agreed that arching my back suited me much better.

I was very pleased with myself. This acting seemed to be most enjoyable. "I'm quite looking forward to my performance," I said.

★

That evening, as soon as Prissy was safely in her room, Miles came to find me. I would never have allowed anyone but him to dust me with flour, but I could see that to be a true ghost-cat, the whiter I was, the more terrifying I would be.

"You've got to be creepy," Miles
told me. "Try to look ghostly."

Of course, Miles did not know
that my friends had helped me and
he was most impressed when I
showed him what I could do.

"That's brilliant, Blossom. Really
ace! Come on, now. We'll go and
start."

I have to confess that I am perhaps a little too plump to be truly spooky, but I did my best. I crept into Prissy's room, where the curtains were closed. The first thing I did was arch my back and hiss a little.

"What's that?" Prissy whispered and sat up in bed. The shriek that came out of her mouth was much more banshee-like than anything I could have produced. I suppose I should have stopped there, but I was having fun. Leaping is something I only do in emergencies, because it is too much like hard work for the rounder type of cat. Still, I decided to

try and reach the bed, for a little
supernatural clawing of the duvet. I
flung myself up as high as I could,
and landed next to Prissy's feet. She
jumped out on to the floor and raced
for the landing, leaving me a little
out of breath.

"Auntiee!" she screeched. "Quick! The ghost-cat is here!"

Miles (who must have been peeping round the door) said, "Hide, Blossom! You were terrific, but we daren't let anyone see you now. Go on, behind the curtain."

I was sorry to leave the bed, but I understood that it would spoil our trick if Mum saw me. She'd know who I was, however much flour there was on my fur. No sooner was I safely out of sight than she came into the room, cuddling Prissy.

"Ghost-cat!" Prissy blubbered. "I saw the ghost-cat."

"There, there, lovey-chops," said Mum. "There's no such thing as a ghost-cat. You've had a bad dream.

I'll sing to you till you go to sleep again."

"Wasn't a dream," Prissy cried. "*Was* a ghost-cat. Miles told me."

"Miles, how could you?" Mum sighed. "Fancy making up the kind of story that would scare a little girl. It's very naughty of you. Go to bed at once. Go on."

Some time later, I pushed myself through the cat-flap and went to tell the Cuckoo Square Cats about the evening's adventures.

"Serves her right," said Geejay, when I'd finished my tale.

"An excellent prank!" Perkins agreed.

"I think you're very brave," said Callie. "I shouldn't like to have flour all over me."

"Miles brushed it off," I said. "Then I licked the bits he left behind. And I can tell you, it's not nearly as nasty-tasting as talcum-powder!"

4. The Last Straw

The next day was Saturday. It was
very hot. The sun burned down from
the sky, and the Cuckoo Square
Cats were lying under the bushes,
looking as limp as kippers on a grill.

"I'm going home," I told them.
"I keep wanting to visit my
water-bowl. Perhaps I shall come
out again after sunset."

"I would go home," said Perkins, "if only I could summon up the energy to cross the Square."

I made my way to the patio, and stretched myself out in a deep shadow. The paving-stones were warm, and soon I was fast asleep. I was woken by someone's foot poking into my side. Miles and Mum and Dad would never prod a cat with their shoe. It was Prissy.

She bent down and said, "I know it was you. You were the ghost-cat. Auntie said. She found flour all over the floor. So, yah boo and sucks to you!"

She prodded me again and wandered off. I should have run away, but the thought of walking all the way to the Square made me feel

very sleepy. I couldn't see Prissy
anywhere, so I closed my eyes again,
and fell into a deep sleep. Suddenly,
a flood of icy water slooshed over
me, drenching my fur, making me
shiver and quiver.

I looked up, terrified, and there was Prissy with a watering-can in her hand, and a nasty little smirk on her face. I hissed loudly, and spat at her, and shook myself. If there's one thing I cannot bear, it's being damp in any way. Once, when I was a tiny kitten, I fell into a sink full of washing-up water and I have had a fear of wetness ever since. I began to walk towards her.

"Prissy, you beast," Miles shouted. He pulled the watering-can out of her hands. "Look what you've done to Blossom. You're so horrible! You're the most horrible person I've ever met and I wish you'd never come to stay! I wish you'd go away!"

"She jumped on my bed!" Prissy

whined. "She scared me, so there!
Serves her right."

"Give me that watering-can,"
Miles yelled, and he pulled it out of
Prissy's hand. Then he ran to
comfort me, just as Mum and Dad
burst out through the French
windows to see what all the noise
was about.

"It's Miles," Prissy whined. "It's him. He's poured water on Blossom and he says I did! Look, he's holding the watering-can."

"I took it away from her," Miles said. "She would have watered poor Blossom again. You know I wouldn't hurt her."

Prissy burst into tears.

"Now, now, Prissy," said Mum. "Stop crying. It couldn't have been Miles, so it must have been an accident. Did you mean to water the flowers and get Blossom instead?"

"Yes," said Prissy. "Blossom was in the way."

Mum said to Miles, "Take Blossom inside and dry her with a

kitchen-towel. Now, Prissy, stop
crying. We'll go and find you some
lovely ice-cream and chocolate
sauce. You'd like that, wouldn't you,
petal?"

They disappeared into the house
and Miles picked me up and took me
to the garage.

"What do you think we can do, Blossom, to make Auntie Iris and Uncle Cliff take her away? Mum and Dad don't think there's anything wrong with her."

I purred at him, and because he understands exactly what all my sounds mean, he knew I was saying, "We'll think of something, don't worry."

Geejay was in the Square later that evening, when I went for a stroll. I told him what had happened.

"I think," said Geejay, "that drastic action is called for. I think I can help you, Blossom. I know something that most humans hate, and run away from . . ."

"Tell me," I said. He whispered in my ear.

When I heard what Geejay was planning, I began to plot my revenge. Prissy would scream, I was quite sure. I couldn't wait for her to catch sight of the surprise that Geejay and I had in store for her.

5. Goodbye, Prissy!

Sunday was even hotter than
Saturday. Perkins, Callie and I had
found a spot in the heart of a
rhododendron bush where the sun
couldn't reach us, and we were lying
there asleep because the weather was
unsuitable for lively conversation.
There was no sign of Geejay. I think
I might have stayed there all day,

but my hunger got the better of me. It always does, especially on a Sunday, when Mum makes delicious roasts for lunch.

"Goodbye," I said to my friends. "It's lamb today, I think."

"My people," said Perkins, "are having salad. It is fortunate that I am not much interested in food."

"He's a fussy eater," Callie whispered to me.

I made my way into my own garden.

"Psst!" whispered a familiar voice. It was Geejay. "Here I am, Blossom."

"Hello, Geejay. Have you got one?"

"Of course," said Geejay. "Here he is. A perfect little mouse with not a mark on him. Just one gentle swipe of my paw and he was out for the count."

"Thank you," I said. "You're a most excellent hunter, Geejay. I don't know what I'd do without you."

"It's a pleasure," said Geejay and went off through the fence at the bottom of our garden.

I am not a good hunter. The thought of chasing things makes me feel tired. The Randalls have been excellent providers of food for years and years, and I've never been a cat to go tearing through the grass and bushes after small creatures who always manage to run faster than I

do. I can't see the point of getting
my paws muddy and my fur ruffled
for something that's no more than a
snack. I pushed Geejay's mouse from
one paw to the other for a while,
and he lay about looking as dead
. . . well, as dead as an exceedingly
dead mouse. I could smell the lamb
cooking and I felt hungrier than
ever. For a moment or two, I
wondered where I could put my prey
so that Prissy would see him and be
scared out of her wits. I hoped this
mouse would be the last straw and
persuade our visitor that she didn't
want to stay with us any longer.

Dad and Miles and Prissy were
sitting at the table. I could see them
from the kitchen door. Mum was

getting ready to pass food through the hatch from the kitchen to the dining-room. She was busy slicing lamb and arranging it on white plates. Next to the lamb, she put some round scoops of mashed potato, and some green beans.

"Come and get these, dear," she called to Dad.

I knew one of the plates was Prissy's. Nobody was looking at me. I moved more quickly than I had done for a long time and dropped the dead mouse into the little valley between two mashed potato mountains. I had a daydream about what would happen . . . Prissy would lift the mouse to her lips with her fork, and possibly even bite on it

before she knew what she was
doing . . .

"There you are, Prissy," said Dad.
"This plate's for you."

"I like mashed potato," she said.
"It's my best thing."

"There you are, then," said Dad.
"Look, I'll put some gravy on it for
you. You like gravy, don't you?"

He didn't wait for an answer, but picked up the gravy-boat and poured thick, brown liquid all over Prissy's lunch. It ran down the sides of the potatoes and formed a puddle on the plate.

Prissy dug her fork into the potato and lifted it to her mouth.

Either the gravy had magical powers, or the hidden rodent was not as dead as I had thought at first. Whiskers all a-twitch, he sat up on the fork and shook his head about. He had a little spot of mash on his nose and his fur was damp with gravy. He took one look at Prissy and jumped down onto the plate. He scrambled over a pile of green beans and began to paddle in the gravy,

bending down to sip it every now
and then, and looking perkier than
any mouse I'd ever seen.

Prissy shrieked. She shrieked so
loudly that a cup fell off its hook on
the kitchen dresser.

"Mouse! Look, Auntiee!"

Mum came running through from
the kitchen. Prissy leapt from her
chair and sent it flying. She knocked
her plate to the floor as well and
bumped into Mum who just
happened to have Miles's lunch in

her hand. Lamb and potatoes and
beans soared into the air and slid
down the walls. Dad leaped from his
chair. It fell over backwards and
very nearly squashed me flat as I
was running for the shelter of the
sideboard. The mouse flew up and

up and landed on the mantelpiece,
where he scattered all the ornaments
on to the floor. They smashed into a
thousand fragments.

"Oh," cried Mum. "My
ornaments!"

"Calm down, Prissy," said Dad, trying to sound firm. "It's only a very little mouse. Look, I've caught it now and I'm going to take it to the garden, and we'll get you another helping. I can't think where it came from. You're not a hunter, are you, Blossom? Blossom, where have you gone?"

I poked my head out of my hiding-place and meowed.

"There she is," said Miles, and he winked at me. He was trying very hard not to laugh.

Prissy was the colour of a beetroot and damp about the face. "I want my mummee!" she moaned, and whatever anyone said to her, she wouldn't be cheered up.

After ten minutes or so, we heard
them. The words that Miles and I
had been waiting for were spoken at
long last.

"I want to go home! I don't want
to stay here any longer!"

Mum said (rather quickly, I
thought. Could it be she was tiring
of darling little Prissy?), "Come on,
then, dear, we'll go and phone your
parents, though I don't know what
Iris will say . . ."

The room looked as though a small bomb had gone off in it. There wasn't anywhere comfortable for a cat to sit, so I went back to the Square.

"You did it, Blossom!" said Callie. We had just watched the roaring car tear out of the Square, carrying Prissy away with it.

Auntie Iris had arrived within hours, and piled the boot full of her daughter's belongings.

"Were Mum and Dad sorry to see her go?" Perkins asked.

"They made sorry noises," I told them, "but I know Mum was happy to have everything calm again. It was the ornaments that did it, I

think. Mum is very fond of all her things. I think she would have made more of an effort to cheer Prissy up if they hadn't been broken."

"I knew the Mouse Trick would work," said Geejay. "Humans don't seem to like them at all. I can't think why. I find them delicious. My

mouth waters when I think of
Mouse and Mash!"

"Thank you, Geejay," I said . . .
"And thanks to you, too, Perkins and
Callie, for all your help. I must go
and find Miles now. We are going to
celebrate."

I found Miles in his room. He was
sitting up in bed.

"I've got my room back," he said,
patting the duvet. "But I've been
waiting for you. Come on, jump up
here."

I looked at him and blinked.

"Sorry, Bloss," he said. "I know
you hate jumping. I'll pick you up."

He lifted me up gently. The duvet
was squashy and warm, and I began

to tread myself a lovely, soft nest in it, right next to Miles's legs.

"I like my bed," he said, "better than any other bed in the world."

"Especially with me curled up on it," I purred.

Miles understood exactly what I was saying. I know that, because he said the very same thing. "Especially with you curled up on it, Blossom."

I closed my eyes. Tomorrow would be a wonderfully peaceful, quiet day. I could feel it in my whiskers.

THE END